a minedition book

North American edition published 2014 by Michael Neugebauer Publishing Ltd. Hong Kong

Illustrations Copyright © 2009 Lisbeth Zwerger
German text by Renate Raecke, English text by Anthea Bell
Rights arranged with "minedition" Rights and Licensing AG, Zurich, Switzerland.
Michael Neugebauer Publishing Ltd., Unit 23, 7F, Kowloon Bay Industrial Centre,
15 Wang Hoi Road, Kowloon Bay, Hong Kong. e-mail: info@minedition.com
This book was printed in April 2014 at L.Rex Printing Co Ltd 3/F., Blue Box Factory Building,
25 Hing Wo Street, Tin Wan, Aberdeen, Hong Kong, China
Typesetting in Veljovic
Library of Congress Cataloging-in-Publication Data available upon request.

ISBN 978-988-8240-82-1

10 9 8 7 6 5 4 3 2 1 First impression

For more information please visit our website: www.minedition.com

THE PIED PIPER
OF HAMELIN

Illustrated by Lisbeth Zwerger

Retold by Renate Raecke from an old legend

collected by Jacob and Wilhelm Grimm

Translated by Anthea Bell

minedition

Hundreds of years ago the people of Hamelin, a town on the river Weser, lived a comfortable, prosperous life. The mills down by the water turned busily, the townsfolk had plenty of flour and bread, vegetables and fish to take to market. Day after day passed by – the good citizens of Hamelin had not a care in the world – and they couldn't imagine this happy state of affairs ever coming to an end.

But one day the rats arrived!

At first only a few rats came, enticed by all the delicious things to eat in the houses of Hamelin, but soon there were more and more of them.

In a very short time, the streets were swarming with those greedy rodents. People hardly dared step out of their doors. The rats even made their way into the kitchens and cellars. Fear and anger filled the town, and worst of all, no one had any idea how to get rid of such a great plague of rats.

One day in the year 1284 – so the old legend says – a strange man appeared in Hamelin. He was a striking figure, wearing a parti-colored or "pied" robe such as the townspeople had never seen before. The story tells us that his name was Bundting. He said he was a rat-catcher, and he promised that, in return for a good fee, he would rid the town of Hamelin of that plague of rats.

Oh, how anxious the good folk of Hamelin were to please the stranger! They begged and implored him to help them, promising him as much gold as he wanted if only he would rid them of the rats. Before long they had struck a bargain with him.

The Mayor himself gave his word of honor that the rat-catcher would be paid the promised fee.

Next day the rat-catcher walked down the streets of the town. He had taken a pipe out of his sleeve, and on it he played a tune that had never been heard before. All over town he went, up streets and down alleys, and wherever his music was heard the rats came scurrying out of kitchens and cellars, storerooms and stables, to follow the Pied Piper. When he thought that not a single rat was left behind, he led the procession out of the town gates and down to the river Weser. He enticed the rats into the water. The current washed them down into the depths, and they all drowned miserably.

How relieved the people of Hamelin were to be rid of that plague of rats! But they were already wishing they hadn't promised the rat-catcher so much gold. Why, it had been child's play for him! All he had needed was his pipe! So they made all kinds of excuses, and wouldn't give him the gold he had earned. The Pied Piper left town in a bitter, angry mood.

But soon after that – on the twenty-sixth of June, the legend says – he returned, dressed like a huntsman, with a big red hat. There was fury in his eyes, and he wanted his revenge. Once again he took his pipe from his sleeve and began playing a strange melody. The people of Hamelin had never heard anything like that tune before.

But while the devout townsfolk prayed in church, the Piper walked the streets of Hamelin once more – and a strange thing happened. All the children who were old enough to walk ran out of the houses and crowded into the streets, just as the rats had done before them. They followed the magical notes of the pipe, blindly trusting the Piper. They surrounded him and ran after him without once looking back. The Mayor's own daughter was among them, although she was really too old for children's games. Yet again, the Pied Piper stepped out through the town gates, and he led the crowd to a mountain near the town, where he and the children all disappeared.

A nursemaid had seen what happened, as she followed the Piper's procession at a distance, with a baby in her arms, but then she turned back and brought the dreadful news to town. Only two children, says the old story, returned to Hamelin. One was blind, and he could tell the townsfolk what he had heard, but he couldn't show them where the Piper had led the children. The other child was deaf and mute, and she could point to the mountain, but she couldn't say what had happened there.

The sorrowful parents hurried out of town to search for their lost children. All the mothers and fathers were weeping and wailing. Messengers were sent out by water and on land to look for any trace of the children, but in vain.

In all, a hundred and thirty children from the town of Hamelin disappeared that day.

And that is the end of the mysterious tale of the disappearance of the children of Hamelin. Ever after, no one was allowed to play music in the street along which the Pied Piper had lured the crowd of children out of town – or so the brothers Jacob and Wilhelm Grimm tell us in their version of the legend.

Even when a newly married couple left church to the sound of fiddles and pipes after their wedding, the musicians had to stop playing their instruments as the bridal procession went down that street. No one was even allowed to beat a drum there, and so the narrow alley was given the name Drumless Street.

AFTERWORD

*There has been much speculation about the background to the legend of the Pied
Piper, which is among the best-known stories collected by the Grimm brothers,
published in a two-volume collection entitled* German Legends *(1816/18).
But to this day, no one has ever discovered for certain what really happened.
In their most famous collection of stories,* Children's and Household Tales, *the
Grimms usually begin with the vague phrase, "Once upon a time …," but in this legend
the brothers give two exact dates telling us when the children left Hamelin: it was in
the year 1284, and even a day, June 26th, according to the Grimms the "Feast of St.
John and St. Paul." Historians have been fascinated by this mention of a specific date,
and by the handwritten entry, in an old chronicle of the town of Hamelin, recording
the children's disappearance – although it is thought to have been added decades after
the event. Not until very much later was the disappearance of the children linked with
the tale of the rat-catcher or Pied Piper.*

*So there are still many unanswered questions, providing much room for myths to
spring up. All the legend itself says is that the Pied Piper led the troop of children
"to a mountain near the town, where he disappeared with them."*

*The phrasing is so vague that it was bound to lead to speculation. One of the
interpretations considered feasible today claims that a "recruiting agent" took the
children away to work in more easterly parts of Europe, which were sparsely inhabited
at the time, and they set off in the direction of Brandenburg or Transylvania.
But another variant suggests they went away by ship to find a new home; Hamelin
owed its economic prosperity to the large number of watermills by the Weser, which is
a navigable river. Other sources again interpret the disappearance of the children as
a journey from which there is no return – meaning that the town suffered an attack of*

the plague which robbed it of a hundred and thirty children at once. The custom was for those who died of the plague to be buried outside the town walls (that could explain the "mountain near the town"), and people avoided saying publicly that their town had suffered an epidemic of the disease, for such an admission would inevitably do harm to the local economy; merchants and traders would have avoided the place for fear of infection.

So the story of the Pied Piper, which has been retold in many literary versions all over the world, remains a mysterious legend to the present day.

Renate Raecke

Other titles illustrated by Lisbeth Zwerger and published by Michael Neugebauer Publishing (minedition) are:

THE LITTLE MERMAID · H.C. Andersen
THE NIGHT BEFORE CHRISTMAS · Clement Clarke Moore
THE BREMEN TOWN MUSICIANS · Jacob and Wilhelm Grimm
NOAH'S ARK · Heinz Janisch
THE SWINEHERD · H.C. Andersen
TALES OF HANS CHRISTIAN ANDERSEN
THE BEST of LISBETH ZWERGER (Art Exhibition Catalogue 2010)

Read more about Lisbeth Zwerger and her books at: www.minedition.com